THE
SHADOW
KILLER

THE SHADOW KILLER

GAIL BOWEN

RAVEN BOOKS
an imprint of
ORCA BOOK PUBLISHERS

Library and Archives Canada Cataloguing in Publication

Bowen, Gail, 1942-
The shadow killer / Gail Bowen.
(Rapid reads)

Issued also in electronic formats.
ISBN 978-1-55469-876-9

I. Title. II. Series: Rapid reads
PS8553.O8995S53 2011   C813'.54   C2011-903438-7

First published in the United States, 2011
Library of Congress Control Number: 2011929021

Summary: Late-night radio host Charlie D has only
two hours to find a troubled young boy and then convince him
not to kill his father and the rest of his family. (RL 5.0)

MIX
Paper from
responsible sources
FSC® C016245

*Orca Book Publishers is dedicated to preserving the environment and has
printed this book on paper certified by the Forest Stewardship Council®.*

Orca Book Publishers gratefully acknowledges the support for
its publishing programs provided by the following agencies:
the Government of Canada through the Canada Book Fund and the
Canada Council for the Arts, and the Province of British Columbia
through the BC Arts Council and the Book Publishing Tax Credit.

Design by Teresa Bubela
Cover photography by Getty Images

ORCA BOOK PUBLISHERS
PO Box 5626, Stn. B
Victoria, BC Canada
V8R 6S4

ORCA BOOK PUBLISHERS
PO Box 468
Custer, WA USA
98240-0468

www.orcabook.com
Printed and bound in Canada.

14 13 12 11 • 4 3 2 1

For Finn, a boy who stands in no one's shadow

CHAPTER ONE

When the sun goes down, the only people on the streets of the neighborhood where I work are people who have something to sell. The women who stroll in skimpy outfits and platform shoes with five-inch heels sell love. Or what passes for love in the dark. The tattooed men in wife-beater shirts, ripped jeans and scuffed black combat boots sell drugs that take their clients up, down or out. Wherever they need to go to dull the pain of being alive.

I'm in the pain-dulling business too. What I offer is a voice that helps people get through the dark hours. My name is Charlie Dowhanuik. I host "The World According to Charlie D"—the late-night call-in show on CVOX radio ("ALL TALK/ ALL THE TIME").

I started out as the midnight deejay. When people began phoning in to talk about their lives, my producer and I decided to cut down on the tunes and focus on the voices.

It was a solid decision. Now we just use tunes to fill the gap between stories. I'm not a shrink or a social worker. The only special skill I have is that I know how to listen. People are hungry for that.

Most nights I ride my bike to work. But the city is in the middle of a heat wave, so tonight I'm on foot. The pavement beneath my feet is soft with heat. The stench of rotting garbage hangs heavy in the air.

It's not a pleasant walk, but this is my neighborhood. And as I pass by, the hookers and drug dealers mumble greetings. I mumble back.

One of the girls calls out, "Happy Father's Day, Charlie."

"I'm not a father," I say.

"If you ever decide you want to make a little Charlie junior, I'm available," she says. Her laugh is a bray.

The first fingers of a headache reach up from the back of my neck into my skull. Aspirin time.

Our local drugstore is grim. Its windows are crisscrossed with protective bars. Several signs announce security cameras and warn that there is minimal cash on the premises.

Tonight there's something new: a sign with a picture of a fancy set of golf clubs and a reminder that says *Don't forget Dad on His Special Day*. Ours is not a neighborhood where people have reason to remember

Dad on his special day. Or on any other day. Most people in this part of town would be hard-pressed to identify their dads in a police lineup.

But inside the store, the greeting-card racks are bright with images of fathers and sons doing what fathers and sons are supposed to do together—play baseball, shoot hoops, catch fish, golf. When I try to remember if I ever did any of those things with my own father, I come up empty. My eyes move to the metal security mirror overhead and I see myself. For thirty-three years, I've lived with the wine-dark birthmark that covers half my face. Mirrors have never been my friends, but my image, distorted by the shiny convex curve of metal, stuns me. I look as if I'm wearing a blood mask. My reflection has caught the attention of a child whose mother is checking out the greeting cards.

The boy is perhaps four years old. He stares at the security mirror for a few seconds, and then his gaze shifts to me. His eyes widen, and he draws near to get a better look. His mother is a dishy redhead with a tennis tan, very brief white shorts and a white T-shirt that showcases her considerable assets. Everything about her shouts money and privilege. What she's doing in this store is a mystery.

When she notices her son staring at me, she hisses, "Don't stare at the man. It's not appropriate."

"He's got blood all over his face," the boy shouts—his voice is high and piercing.

Quick as the flick of a snake's tongue, the mother reaches out a perfect hand and slaps her son's cheek. He howls.

I meet her gaze.

"*That* wasn't appropriate," I say. As I walk over to the cashier and take my place in line, I feel the perfect redhead's eyes boring a hole in the back of my head.

There's a stack of local newspapers on the counter by the cashier. I pick one up. For once, there is something new in the news. Two photos share pride of place on the front page. The first is of a man and a woman in evening clothes. His name is Henry Burgh; her name is Misty de Vol. They are beaming at one another with the satisfaction of two people who have found what they want out of life. He is a tough-looking old bird of eighty-three; she is a curvy blond of twenty-five. The photograph is their engagement picture.

The second photograph is of a man with a three-hundred-dollar haircut, hard eyes and a snarl for a smile. His name is Evan Burgh. He owns the network of which CVOX is the crown jewel. Henry, the groom-to-be, is his father.

For the past month, there've been whispers that before Henry has a chance to make Misty his bride, Evan Burgh will attempt to have the courts declare that his father's "best before" date has expired. The headline above the pictures tells the tale: *DAD'S IN LA-LA-LAND SAYS SON*. It appears that Evan's first kick at the can is to go public. I've locked horns with him enough times to know that he's a prick, so I'm on the side of young love.

The paper's other stories are the usual—a gang murder, an armed robbery, the threat of a garbage strike. There's a shot of the rising star in the political party my father led for many years. Rising Star is barbecuing ribs for his family. The wife and kids look as if they'd rather be eating ground glass than sharing a family moment with Dad. Mrs. Rising Star's smile is frozen. The faces of the two pretty teenage daughters are grim. And the third child, a boy on the cusp of adolescence, is staring down at the picnic table, his face expressionless.

Only Leader Dad is beaming, clearly oblivious to his wife and kids. Although he has proposed slashing programs for youth at risk, single mothers and the working poor, he is being packaged as a proud protector of families. Not my kind of guy. But I look hard at the picture, especially at the boy.

My father, Howard Dowhanuik, was a politician—a successful one. I grew up being dragged into family publicity photos. Nobody wanted a gap in the picture where the third child should be.

The camera was not kind to the supporting cast of the Dowhanuik family. My activist-mother always looked as if she couldn't wait to break away and do something meaningful. My beautiful sisters flashed smiles that were clearly fake, and my birthmark made me look as if

I belonged to some bizarre face-painting cult. But the camera loved my father. Bathed in the glow of the successful politician, he always looked great. And why not? Howard Dowhanuik was the king of the castle, the people's choice.

I pay for the paper and the aspirin and leave the store. When I turn at the corner, I see the fluorescent call letters on the roof of the radio station. The *O* in CVOX is an open red-lipped mouth with a tongue that looks like Mick Jagger's. It may be cheezy, but it's the beacon that leads me to the place that is the closest thing to home I know.

As I step through the glass doors that open into the station's foyer, my cell phone vibrates. I check the caller ID. It's my father. He makes an effort to contact me three times a year—once each on the anniversaries of the death of my mother and of the woman I loved, and once close to Father's Day. After a life in politics, Howard knows how to turn the knife.

I drop the cell back in my pocket, pass through security and make my way down a hall hung with over-sized photographs of CVOX's heavy hitters. "The World According to Charlie D" is our station's top-rated show, so my picture, taken in profile to feature my "good side," is front and center. I'm proud of our show. I think we do good work, but there are nights when I feel as if I'm swimming upstream. I look again at the newspaper in my hand and my spidey senses begin to tingle. That's when I know that even though it's still ten minutes to showtime, I'm already in over my head.

CHAPTER TWO

When I enter the brightly lit control room of Studio D, Nova Langenegger, who has produced the show since the beginning, is keying something into her computer. She has a phone balanced between her ear and her shoulder. In the year since her daughter, Lily, was born, Nova has started running. I thought she looked fine with a few extra pounds, but she didn't share my opinion.

She's my age, but tonight, with her blond hair tied up in a ponytail and her runner's body in a tank top and shorts, she looks about seventeen. Nova never wears makeup. She doesn't need to. Her skin is creamy and taut, and her eyes are the intense blue of an Alpine sky. Her steady gaze has rescued me more than once over the years.

Nova is not easily rattled, but she can't take her eyes off whatever's on her computer screen.

"Look at this." She points to an email.

I lean over her shoulder and read the words aloud. *"For all of us, being dead would be better than living with him. When Charlie said 'no man is a man until his father dies,' I knew what I had to do."*

"No name," she says. "Just an email address. Loser1121@anonymous.org."

There's a coldness in the pit of my stomach. After ten years, I can tell when someone is about to cross the blood-red line. I keep my voice even.

"Did I say that?"

Nova's fingernails are already chewed to the quick, but she slides what remains of her thumbnail into her mouth and nods.

"You did. I checked through the tapes for the last six weeks and found the exact words." She adjusts the elastic on her ponytail. "The topic was guilt. The caller's name was Brian, and he was beating himself up because his father died, and all he felt was relief."

"I remember," I say. "That voice is pretty hard to forget. Brian sounded as if he was being torn apart by the hounds of hell."

"It wasn't any easier listening to him the second time," Nova says dryly. "I jotted down the key points of your conversation." She picks up a scratch pad and begins reading. "Brian said, 'A man's supposed to cry for his father, but I can't cry. I just keep feeling relieved that he's finally gone.' You tried a couple of approaches, but you weren't connecting. Finally, you reached

13

into your Tickle Trunk of a brain and came up with something that worked. 'Fathers cast long shadows,' you said. 'It's easy to get lost in them.'"

"That's when Brian started listening," I said. "I told him about an article I'd read. The writer believed fathers become an audience of one for their sons."

Nova reads from her scratch pad.

"'Fathers teach their sons how to throw a ball, and then they watch and cheer. A boy grows up knowing that his dad's always going to be in the stands, watching.'"

"Which is great unless the boy becomes a man who is still always trying to please that audience of one," I say.

"And that's where the fatal quote came in." Nova consults her scratch pad again and reads. "'The son who is always trying to please his father will never be a man until the father dies.'"

I rub the back of my neck. The aspirin has not yet worked its magic. I watch Nova's face carefully.

"Would you interpret that as me giving someone license to kill his father?"

Nova's smile is thin.

"No. I'd interpret that as you telling Brian that he isn't a monster—that other people have reacted to a father's death the way he has. But people hear what they want to hear."

"And loser1121 wanted to hear that he'd be justified in killing his father."

Nova's face is tense. "Not just his father. The email reads 'For all of us, being dead would be better than living with him.' Charlie, I think loser1121 is planning to kill everyone in his family, including himself."

I feel as if someone just dropped a large barbell on the back of my neck.

"So where do we go from here?" I say.

"Your decision," Nova says. "Since I came to work tonight, I've had two hang-ups. I usually take that as an indication the caller wants to talk to you." Her brow furrows. "Do you think it's time to alert the police?"

I shrug. "We might as well cover our asses. But I can tell you right now what they'll say. 'The World According to Charlie D' is broadcast coast to coast. All we have is an email address. Loser1121 could be anywhere. No police force in the country has the time or the resources to search for a needle in a haystack. Then they'll say we have to get loser1121 to call in so we can either talk him down or trace the call." I rub my skull and wince.

Nova narrows her eyes. "Your Father's Day headache started early this year," she says. "While we're on the subject... your father called. He's across the street at Nighthawks. He wants to come over after the show and take you for coffee."

"Not going to happen," I say.

After ten years together, Nova and I know each other's stories. Her mother died of cancer when Nova was five. She had two younger sisters. Her father ran the farm, cooked, ironed the girls' church dresses, and when the time came, he sat them down with a box of sanitary napkins and explained menstruation. When he died at fifty-two, he left behind three smart, self-reliant young women who still mourn him.

Nova's eyes search my face. Clearly, she's concerned about what she sees. "I have something for you," she says. "I was going to give it to you after the show, but you look as if you could use it now." She reaches into her backpack and takes out an eight-by-ten-inch photograph of her year-old daughter, Lily. Lily is wearing overalls and blowing the fluff off the dandelion she's clutching in her hand.

I look at the photo for a long time.

"She is so beautiful," I say.

"Agreed," Nova says. "Medical student number seven must have been a hunk. First time at the sperm bank, and I hit the jackpot."

"Don't sell yourself short," I say. "Lily's like you in many ways."

The picture has been professionally framed. To set off the photograph, Nova chose a navy mat that matches Lily's overalls. There are tiny white handprints on the navy mat.

"How did you get Lily's handprints on there?" I ask.

Nova rolls her eyes.

"With white paint and great difficulty," she says. "There's a verse on the back, but don't read it while I'm around. I don't want to watch your opinion of me take a nosedive."

She glances at the big clock above the glass that faces my studio. "Two minutes to air," she says. "There are some notes for the opening on your screen. I'll call the police, but I think you're right about their response. They'll need more to go on, and we're the only ones who can get it. I'm going to answer loser1121's email—urge him to give us a call on air or off. But, Charlie, you'll have to be the point guy on this."

I nod agreement. "And I'll have to tread lightly. This guy is hanging on by his toenails. The last thing we want to do is freak him out."

I pass from the bright light of the control room into the dark coolness of my studio. I slide into my seat at the desk and pick up my earphones. Nova's notes for the intro are on my computer screen, but I don't read them. I turn over the photograph she gave me and read the verse written on the back.

You sometimes get discouraged because I am
*   so small*
And always get my fingerprints on furniture
*   and wall.*
So here's a final handprint so that you
*   can recall*
How very much I loved you when my hands
*   were just this small.*

My throat closes. When we're at our desks, Nova and I communicate through hand signals and our talkback microphone. I don't trust my voice, so I give Nova the thumbs-up.

She leans forward and switches on her talkback. "Don't get emotional," she says. "It was either you or medical student number seven." Her tone is ironic, but her crooked grin would melt a heart harder than mine. She holds up five fingers and counts down. We're on the air.

CHAPTER THREE

Our theme music, "Ants Marching" by the Dave Matthews Band, comes up. When the music fades, it's my turn.

There's an old joke: "He has a great face for radio." In my case, it's true. I started doing radio because it allowed me to be somebody I wasn't. Like everyone in my business, I've developed a voice that works for my audience. Charlie D's voice is deep, intimate and confiding—the voice of the man women want to go home with them after midnight. The voice of the man other men wish they could be.

It was a kick when the fan mail started. Reading that a woman found listening to my voice like being bathed in dark honey was an ego boost. But when people began to write that my voice was all that got them through the night, I knew that "The World According to Charlie D" wasn't about me. That's when I started taking the show seriously.

I glance at my computer screen. Most nights Nova sketches out an intro for me, but loser1121 has distracted her. Always professional, she's left me some Internet quotes about fatherhood to riff on.

My eyes scan the page. Bill Cosby says, *Fatherhood is pretending the present you love most is soap-on-a-rope.* The philosopher Friedrich Nietzsche gives wise counsel: *When one has not had a good father, one must create one.* Spike Milligan is provocative: *My father had a profound influence on me—he was a lunatic.* There are other quotes, but until the second page, the pickings are slim.

Midway down page two, there's a tasty morsel from Anonymous. *A man's desire for a son is nothing but the wish to duplicate in order that such a remarkable pattern may not be lost to the world.* I read the quote again. Anonymous seems to have hit on yet another reason why I was such a disappointment to my father.

The final quote on the page is dynamite. *Those who have never had a father never know the sweetness of losing one. To most men, the death of the father is a new lease on life...* Samuel Butler.

I know nothing about Samuel Butler, but Google will. I type in his name. There are pages of information, but one fact leaps out at me: Sam was born on December 5, 1835. My birthday is December 5, 1978. Sam and I are birthday twins. And another coincidence: Sam and I both came up with snake-eyes when we rolled the dice in the great Daddy crapshoot.

The music of Dave and his band fades. Time for me to get to work. I lean into my mike and crank up the energy.

"*It's June 20th—Father's Day weekend. Time to reward Dad for services rendered. And there's the rub. When it comes to dads, it's not one-size-fits-all. If your dad's like Ward Cleaver on the old sitcom* Leave It to Beaver, *he deserves the full treatment—a snappy golf shirt, an industrial-sized bottle of Old Spice, a monogrammed tie and a chocolate cake with* World's Best Dad *spelled out in Smarties on the icing. If your dad's more along the lines of Homer Simpson or the Family Guy, he'll welcome a six pack and something to incinerate on the barbecue.*

"*Of course, there are Dad-zillas who don't deserve gifts. In the Greek myth, Kronos ate his own children. No soap-on-a-rope for Kronos. And no A&W Papa Burger for Abraham—who had the knife sharpened to kill his son Isaac, until a ram got his horns stuck in a bush and gave Abraham an option.*

"We don't choose our fathers. The biggest lottery any of us will ever be involved in is the one in which the sperm swims over and knocks on the door of the egg. The moment the egg decides to let Mr. Wiggles in, our life is decided.

"So how did you make out in the Daddy Derby? Did you get a thoroughbred? A plug? A skittish dad who never came out of the gate? Or did you get a dad who streaked out of the gate and never came back? Our lines are open. Give me a call at 1-800-555-2333 or email me at charlied@nationtv.com."

I lower my voice to a level that is intimate and inviting. "Here's a message for one special caller. You sign yourself loser1121, but you're not a loser, and you're not alone. Many or us have learned that Father doesn't always know best. Give yourself a chance. Don't do anything you can't undo. We need to talk. On air or off, your choice—but talking will help."

Time to move the show along. I pick up the energy. "And now here's Harry Chapin

25

with 'Cat's in the Cradle,' a song about a man who discovers too late that fathers pay a price for being too busy for their sons."

Harry Chapin's voice is gentle and tuneful. I open up the talkback. "Anything from loser1121?"

Nova shakes her head. "Nope, but there is news. Which do you want first—the good or the bad?"

"Hit me with the good stuff."

"Aldo just called—Ruby's in hard labor. With luck, the baby will be born when we're on the air."

I feel a jolt of pure joy. I never used to think about the future, but since Nova gave birth to Lily, I think about it a lot. Aldo has been the technician on "The World According to Charlie D" since we started, so this baby will be family. "Everybody okay?" I say.

"So far, so good," Nova replies. "I talked to Ruby. The contractions are three minutes apart. She and I agree that on the utterly unbearable pain scale, childbirth is right up there with a Brazilian bikini wax."

"What's a Brazilian bikini wax?"

Nova's mouth twitches. "Tell you after the show." The fun goes out of her face. "And while we're on the subject of utterly unbearable pain, our first caller tonight is Evan Burgh. There were ten people ahead of him, but, as he reminded me, he does own the network."

"And our show can be replaced," I say.

Nova's lips are tight. "I believe that possibility was mentioned." Her eyes meet mine. "Charlie, don't take on Evan Burgh. He's a snake, and a lot of people count on you."

I glance at my computer screen. "Loser1121 is getting closer to making the big move. Check your inbox, Nova."

Nova lowers her eyes to her screen. Over the talkback, I hear her intake of breath.

"Time to call the cops again?" she asks.

"Yes, and this time we've got something for them."

I look again at loser1121's message: *I've attached a picture of our family carving knife. My father says that the only one who's allowed to use it is the man of the house. Tonight I will become the man of the house.* I open the attachment, and my heart clenches. I'm not an expert, but even I can see that this knife is capable of carving everything the man of the house decides to carve.

CHAPTER FOUR

The ending of "Cat's in the Cradle" is sweet and sour. The father's wish to have his son grow into a man just like him comes true. The boy who once longed for his father's love has become an adult whose busy life has no place for his father. Long ago, I sent my father a tape of Harry Chapin singing "Cat's in the Cradle." I wonder if he ever got it.

The newspaper I bought in the drugstore is on my desk. They say a picture is worth a thousand words. The photograph of Evan Burgh tells you everything you need to know about the man. His face is strained by the knowledge that what he wants will always be beyond his reach. No matter how much money or power or property he has, it will never be enough. His only pleasure comes from making the people around him feel small and scared. Evan's a mean son of a bitch, and I would love to take him on, but tonight loser1121 and his carving knife take precedence.

I inhale deeply, reach for my cool-guy-in-charge voice and flip on my mike. *"And we're back,"* I say. *"You're listening to 'The World According to Charlie D.' Our topic tonight is fathers. Over two thousand years ago, the Roman poet Horace said, 'Rarely are sons similar to their fathers. Most are worse. A few are better.' Something to ponder. Our lines are open. Give us a call at 1-800-555-2333 or email us at charlied@nationtv.com.*

"Our first caller is Evan. So, Evan, what's on your dad's wish list this Father's Day weekend?"

Evan Burgh's voice is high, pompous and tight with anger.

"Read the papers, Charlie D," he says. *"My father is purchasing his own gift. This Sunday, he's marrying Misty de Vol. Ms. de Vol calls herself a model, but for the past three years she's worked for the Five Star Escort Service. She's a hooker."*

"A gift that keeps on giving," I say.

"A gift that keeps on taking." Evan's voice is acid. *"And he's marrying her on Father's Day—one more way to stick the knife into me."*

Somewhere out in radio-land, loser1121 is testing the blade of a real knife and making plans to use it. Generally, I give callers some time to settle in, but Evan is a maggot, and I've already had enough.

"Let's cut to the chase," I say. *"Evan, why did you call in tonight?"*

There is a crispness to Evan's pronunciation, as if he is showing the rest of us how to speak the language.

"*Because I want the world to know my father is an ass,*" he says. "*He's eighty-three years old. What in the name of God is he going to do with a twenty-five-year-old sex worker?*"

"*Come on, Evan,*" I say. "*Somewhere along the line, Dad must have talked to you about what consenting adults do behind closed doors.*"

Evan's snicker is ugly.

"*Thanks to the media, I know only too well what my father and Ms. de Vol do behind closed doors. The tabloids have been graphic in describing the smorgasbord of sexual delights Ms. de Vol offers her customers.*"

"*And you think your father is marrying Ms. de Vol simply to gratify himself.*"

"*I don't give a damn why he's marrying her. I'm just curious about the mental capability of a man who signs a prenuptial agreement with a whore, guaranteeing her ten million dollars for every year of their marriage. Until she met my father, Ms. de Vol's rate was eight hundred* dollars an hour with a two-hour minimum. From eight hundred an hour to ten million a year. That's quite a pay hike for a prostitute."

"Your father is a billionaire," I say. "It'll take the newlyweds years to run through all that money."

"You're missing the point," Evan says. His voice is icy with contempt.

I grit my teeth.

"Maybe I am missing the point," I say. "Why don't you help me out, Evan? When I listen to you, what I hear is a preening turd with millions of dollars, and more on the way when Daddy dies, complaining because his father has found some pleasure in life. If there's more, tell me. If there's not, take Dad out for a beer, air your differences privately and let me get on with what you're paying me to do—help people with real problems get through the night."

"You work for me, Charlie. You do what I tell you to do." He spits out the words.

I slam my fist into my palm but remain silent. Nova's back is rigid with tension. Since Evan came on the line, she's been watching me, waiting for a signal. Now I give it. I draw my finger across my throat in the slashing sign that indicates it's time to cut off the caller.

"Fire me," I say. *"And Evan, if you call in again, you're going to have to go to the end of the line and wait your turn. 'The World According to Charlie D' has a policy of zero tolerance for bullies."*

"You'll regret this," he says.

"There's a lot I regret," I say, *"but telling you to take a hike will never be in my top ten. Now here's a tune for you, Evan—the Beach Boys with 'I'm Bugged At My Ol' Man.'"*

As the Beach Boys sing about a boy who comes home a little late and is confronted by a dad who grounds him, sells his surfboard, cuts off his hair while he's sleeping, pulls his phone out of the wall and rips up his clothes, I find myself hoping that Evan is still listening. Henry Burgh may be marrying a hooker, but at least he didn't sell his son's surfboard.

CHAPTER FIVE

When I see the name of the next caller, I want to give Fate a standing ovation. Britney is a regular. She's that rarest of adolescents: a teenager whose life is uncomplicated. Brit sent me her school picture, and she's a beauty. She's also smarter than she lets on. And—the cherry on the cheesecake—she's surrounded by people who love her. She calls in to "The World According to Charlie D" because she likes to hear her voice on the radio. We take her calls because her understanding of others is surprisingly solid.

"Hey, wild child," I say. "What's on your mind tonight?"

Britney's laugh is a waterfall. "Oh, Charlie, I love it when you call me 'wild child'—as if I ever did anything really wild or even semi-wild. Anyway, I know you're mad at Evan. He's your boss—right? All that stuff about firing you? It's not going to happen. Evan's just upset, and I know why. Nobody likes to think about their parents actually doing it. It's just too gross."

I gaze down at the newspaper photo of the political Rising Star and his tightly wound wife. Hard to imagine those two doin' the crazy. Just as well, because their kids already look as if they're ready to spontaneously combust.

Britney is rattling away.

"It must be supergross for Evan because his dad is, like, eighty-three. But all the same, if his dad has found a girl who's willing to...you know...do it with him, I think it's great."

I relax.

"*Ah, Brit, you're such a romantic.*"

Her voice grows serious.

"*I may be a romantic, but I'm not stupid. I know what an escort is. But if the old gentleman wants to pay a lady to make him happy, why not? It's always like that with girls and guys. It's up to the girl to decide. If a guy takes me to like a really stellar classic concert— like, say, Rihanna—he's going to expect some- thing. It's up to me to decide whether he gets it. Guys know this and girls know it. What's the difference? Coming across for Rihanna—which I absolutely would not do, incidentally—or coming across for ten million dollars a year...which is really a lot...*" For a moment, the possibilities of a check with all those zeroes mesmerizes Brit. Her voice trails off.

I bring her back to earth.

"*So you're cool with Evan's father marrying Misty.*"

"*Absolutely. My grandma always says, 'There are no pockets in a shroud,' and she's right.*"

Britney's voice grows solemn. *"I would just like to say that I wish Henry and Misty every happiness."*

"You're a good person, Britney," I say, and I mean it.

Time to move back into Charlie-D mode.

"So there you have it," I say. *"Our resident romantic, Britney, has given the soon-to-be newlyweds her blessing. I'd like to add my good wishes. Henry and Misty, here's to you. May you live happily ever after.*

"Next up...a first-time caller whose name is..." On my computer screen, there's a blank where the name should be. I shoot Nova a questioning glance.

She lowers her eyes and opens her talkback.

"Just take the call," she says. Nova would never make a poker player. Her tone is no-nonsense, but she can't stop beaming.

I shrug and open my mike.

"O-kay, so our first-time caller's identity is a mystery, but hey, life's a mystery. Our topic tonight is fathers. If you have thoughts on the subject, give us a call at 1-800-555-2333 or email us at charlied@nationtv.com.

"So, Caller X, time for you to join the party. How did you make out in the great Daddy Derby?" For a beat there's silence, and then I hear the ear-splitting, surprisingly lusty cry of a newborn.

I open my talkback to Nova.

"Is that who I think it is?" She nods and gives me a bullet-stopping grin.

On the line there is muffled laughter. Then I hear the gravelly voice I've heard through my headset since the night I started at CVOX. *"Hey, Charlie, you were just talking to my son—Aldo Patrick DeLuca Junior. The kid's got lungs, eh?"*

Again, I find my throat closing—not a good thing in my business. Genuine emotion is the enemy of talk-radio hosts.

"Yeah," I say. *"The kid's definitely got his father's lungs. For those of you who don't know him—that's the voice of our technician, Aldo DeLuca. He's the guy who makes it possible for you out there and us in here to communicate. So, Aldo, when did your son make his appearance?"*

"Two minutes ago—he didn't want to miss his debut on 'The World According to Charlie D.'"

"So the kid's a trooper. Speaking of troopers...how's Ruby?"

"Great. Beautiful. She won't let me take pictures of her until she fixes her mascara—which is impossible because she's so happy she can't stop crying. I'm crying too. So's Aldo Junior. We're the happiest people on earth."

I laugh. *"Keep it up."*

"We will. Hey, Charlie, I heard what you read earlier about how a lot of sons are worse than their fathers. I just want to say that this isn't going to happen with me and Aldo Junior.

I'm going to do everything in my power to make my son a better man than me."

He chokes, and when he returns, Aldo's voice is husky with emotion.

"I'm outta here," he says. *"When my son listens to the tape of the night he was born, I don't want him to hear me blubbering."*

Aldo is a macho guy. He has a great work ethic, but before he and Ruby got together, Aldo and Nova locked horns over his attitude toward women and the mottos on his T-shirts.

Ruby changed everything. She transformed Aldo from a tough guy into Prince Charming. When Nova was pregnant, Aldo treated her as if she was spun gold. When Ruby became pregnant, Nova hovered over Aldo

In the control booth, Nova is mopping her eyes with a tissue. I check my computer screen. Henry Burgh is next on deck. I take out my bottle of aspirin. Too soon for the next dose, but I leave the bottle on the desk. Sometimes even the promise of relief is a relief.

I shoot Nova a glance, but she's busy keying a message into her computer. The glow has gone from her face. Her body is tense. I check my screen. Henry Burgh is a primo caller, but we're not going to him. We're going to music again. We never have two tunes this close together. Something is not right.

"O-kay," I say. *"Here's a song for Aldo and for all the other guys out there who take their dad-ly duties seriously. It's the Winstons with 'Color Him Father.'"*

I hum a few bars along with the Winstons, and then I turn on my talkback. "Only two callers and we're already doing another tune?" I say. "Are you afraid Henry Burgh is going to turn Misty loose on me?"

Nova is staring at her computer screen. "At the moment, Henry is far from our biggest problem. Loser1121 just emailed his plan for the murders. I'm forwarding it as an attachment." There's a catch in her voice. "Charlie, this is a nightmare."

I open the attachment. It's an architect's blueprint of a house. Loser1121 has marked his route for the killings in red Sharpie. The thick red line starts in the kitchen, goes up a back staircase and then to a large bedroom on the east side of the house. Outlines of twin beds are drawn against one of the walls. Each bed is marked with three letters. I assume they're the initials of the person who sleeps in the bed: *LMK* and *VCK*. On top of each set of initials, loser1121 has drawn a large *X*.

The red line leaves the bedroom and goes down a hallway into a wing on the west side of the house. The blueprint identifies this as the master bedroom. A double bed is drawn against the far wall. At the head of the bed, there are two sets of initials: *MEK* and *JAK*. Both are X'd out. Finally the red line doubles back to the stairs that lead to the third floor. The bed in this loft bedroom is marked with the initials *JJK*. It, too, bears an *X*. Each of the sets of initials is numbered. LMK is number 1; VCK is number 2; MEK is 3; JAK is 4; and JJK is numbered 5. The thick red line stops at JJK's bed. His will be the last blood shed.

CHAPTER SIX

The Winstons' graceful tribute to the stepfather who raised them to be proud and loving men ends. It's my turn now, but I can't move. Through my earphones, I hear dead air—fatal for talk radio. Nova takes over. Her voice is shaky, but she's in charge. "The cops are on their way," she says. "Henry Burgh's on line one. Can you handle him?"

I nod, take a deep breath, dig deep for my cool voice and flip on my microphone. My hands are trembling, but my imitation of the unflappable Charlie D is convincing.

"*Hey, Henry, this is a big night for us. You're a first-time caller and our show's first billionaire. Thanks for joining the party.*"

Henry's bass rumbles with authority, but he's in high spirits.

"*I wanted to thank Britney for her good wishes. Misty's right here with me, and she appreciates Britney's kindness too. People of my generation are often too quick to dismiss young people. They have a great deal to offer.*"

"*Agreed,*" I say. "*You've obviously discovered that Misty has a great deal to offer.*"

Provoking a billionaire is never a sharp move, but Henry takes my comments in stride.

"*Misty is a woman of infinite variety. But enumerating my bride-to-be's many charms would just get me into a pissing match with my son. I've always been able to out-piss Evan.*" He chuckles. "*Besides, Misty is attempting to teach me to turn the other cheek.*"

I find myself liking Henry.

"So how's that working out for you?"

His laugh rumbles.

"Let's just say it's not easy to teach an old dog new tricks."

I turn to share the moment with Nova. What I see makes me reach for the aspirin. The control room is filling with cops. This baffles me. The danger is out there, not in here.

Through the talkback, Nova's voice is tense, but she's in control.

"We're going to another tune. Ask Henry Burgh to stay on the line. If we're going to lure loser1121, we're going to have to bait the hook."

"And Henry will keep the focus where we need it to be—on fathers and sons."

"We can't afford to blow this, Charlie. Do whatever's necessary to keep Henry onside."

I flip my mike back on.

"*Henry, I apologize, we're having some technical difficulties.*"

"*I assumed as much,*" he says. "*Over the years, I've hung up on many people, but no one ever hangs up on me.*"

"*Being a billionaire has its advantages,*" I say. "*Unfortunately, money can't straighten out whatever's playing havoc with our phone lines. We're going to stay with music till we fix the problem. Will you stick around?*"

"*Of course,*" he says. "*At eighty-three, adventures don't come every day. And Misty's always up for adventures, aren't you, my love?*" In the background a woman laughs softly.

I smile to myself. Henry's marriage to Misty de Vol may not be a love match, but Misty knows how to give a man his money's worth. I lean into my microphone.

"*Hey, it appears that gremlins are scrambling our phone lines tonight, so please hold your calls. As our tech works at unscrambling,*" *let's have a listen to Lenny Kravitz singing Elton John's rocking 'Like Father Like Son.'"*

I stretch to get the kinks out, but it's not my night to un-kink. Nova's on the talkback.

"You're fired, Charlie. Check your inbox. Evan Burgh sent a blistering email. He didn't take kindly to you cozying up to his dad."

I shrug. "You know what they say. 'Freedom's just another word for nothin' left to lose.'"

Nova's laugh is thin.

"That's the spirit. Okay, here's the situation. One of the officers in here with me is a psychologist. She thinks loser1121's hatred for his father has been building for a long time. In her opinion, creating the plan was a safety valve for 1121."

"But now the plan doesn't bring the same old thrill," I say.

"No, the police shrink is convinced that 1121 is ready to act. Her colleagues on the force agree that there's no way the authorities can find this kid. He could be anywhere. The initials he's written on the blueprint are useless. So is his email address. Anonymous.org is one of those temporary web-based addresses that don't require registration. You're going to have to get him to call in."

"I'll bet Henry Burgh has a few ideas on the relationship between fathers and sons. I'll see if I can get him to provoke a response from loser1121."

I flip on my mike.

"And we're back. Our first-time caller, Henry Burgh, has been kind enough to stick around. So, Henry, earlier on the show I refer-enced an ancient sage who said that most sons are worse than their fathers. Any thoughts?"

Henry doesn't hesitate.

"I agree," he says flatly. *"It doesn't start out that way. Most of us start out like Aldo. We have big dreams for our sons. They're the*

center of our existence. Then expectations on both sides aren't met. One day a father wakes up and realizes that his son is never going to be the man he dreamed he would be. One day the son wakes up and sees the disappointment in his father's eyes when he looks at him. They both cut their losses. They start avoiding one another. Why put yourself through that pain— on either side? Then the son grows up and does everything he can to spite his father."

I think of my father waiting in a coffee shop for me to finish tonight's show so we can get together and slap a Hallmark ending on thirty-three years of indifference and neglect.

"Is it always the son who's at fault?" I ask, and my mind is no longer on 1121.

"Does it matter?" Henry says. *"The day a father realizes that his son will never be the man he is, the damage is done. It's a Humpty Dumpty thing—once a hope is shattered, it can never be put back together again."*

"What about the son's hopes?"

"That would be the son's problem, wouldn't it?" Henry says. The warmth has gone from his voice. For the first time that night, he sounds a lot like Evan. Maybe Lenny Kravitz had it right. Genes will tell. No matter what a boy does, he's destined to end up like his father.

It's a depressing thought, but I don't have much time to ponder. Nova calls on the talkback. Loser1121 is on line two. I thank Henry, cut him off and open line two.

CHAPTER SEVEN

His voice is a surprise. It's small, high-pitched, edged with doom.

"This is loser1121—I've sent you some emails. Did you get them?"

"I did. Can you tell me your real name?"

"Loser1121 is my real name." His tone is flat, the voice of someone to whom nothing matters. "I tried to be just 'loser' on my email address, but the name was taken. Loser1121 was the first name that was still available. That means there are 1,120 losers ahead of me. I'm not even the first."

His pain at being denied even this small distinction makes me wince.

"*I've felt like a loser for much of my life,*" I say.

Even his laugh is a sob.

"*You're just saying that. I listen to your show every night. You're a winner, Charlie D. People worship you. The kids at my school try to talk like you—edgy, funny, smart. I've tried myself—just at home in my room. I try to make my voice low like yours, but it comes out wrong. Everything I do comes out wrong. But tonight it's going to be different.*"

"*So what are you doing tonight?*"

"*Killing my family,*" he says. His voice is without emotion. He could be announcing that he'll be sitting with a bowl of popcorn watching a DVD. "*Charlie, you know what I'm going to do.*" He raises his voice. He's angry now. "*I sent you the plans. You've been waiting for me to call. That's why you made up all that*" *stuff about problems with the phone lines. There were no problems with the phone lines. When I called, I got right in."*

I try a laugh.

"You're too smart for me."

"Smart enough not to let you stop me." He tries for a tough-guy growl, but in one humiliating adolescent moment, his voice breaks. He's younger than I thought— perhaps as young as thirteen or fourteen.

"I know I can't stop you," I say. *"I was hoping you'd stop yourself."*

"Why? Just to prove one more time that I can't do anything right?"

"Killing your family isn't right," I say.

"You don't know what you're talking about."

Suddenly he sounds confident. I'm losing ground.

"You've only known me a couple of minutes," he says. *"I've known me fourteen years. So have the people in my family. They know I'm a loser. Every time they look at me, I see it in their eyes.*

But after tonight, they'll never have to look at me again."

"Where are you now?"

"Still up on the third floor in my room. You know what comes next. I sent you the blueprint. I'm going downstairs to close my sisters' eyes. Then I'll close my mother's eyes, and then I'll close his eyes."

"Your father's?" I ask.

"Don't do that! You knew who I meant!" His voice cracks. He takes a breath. "Then I'll come back to my room, and that will be the end."

"Please, don't do this," I say. My voice is as weak as my words.

"Too late, Charlie D. It's time to get started. I have my father's knife. But guess what?" His laugh is childlike but haunting. "It's not his knife anymore. It's mine."

My pulse is racing.

"Stay on the line—please." I rack my brain for something—anything—that will keep him from breaking our connection. As long as he's talking to me, he's not killing the members of his family. *"Why did you send me the blueprint?"* I say. *"If you didn't want to be stopped, why did you call in tonight?"*

He doesn't answer. In the silence, I can hear my heart pounding. It's too late. I reach for the bottle of aspirin, shake two into my palm and dry-chew them. It's over.

I start to take off my earphones; then I hear him. His voice is small, and it seems as if it's painful for him to talk.

"I wanted a record," he says. *"I didn't want people to think I was just screwed-up like the two kids who did the Columbine shooting. They were weirdos who were into guns and homemade explosives. I want people to hear my real voice. So they'd know…"*

"So they'd know what?"

Loser1121 is fighting tears, and he isn't winning. He's breaking apart.

"So they'd know that I love my mother and I love my sisters."

"Then why are you going to end their lives?" I ask.

He raises his voice in frustration.

"Because I love them. I just told you that. They've always tried to protect me against him."

"Does your father hurt you physically?"

"Not physically. He has other ways. And my mother and my sisters always tell me my father is wrong about me. They say I'm a good person, a worthwhile person—they believe in me."

"Then why do you want to…to 'close their eyes'?"

"I don't want them to spend the rest of their lives having people look away from them because they're the family with the boy who killed his father."

"So you're killing your mother and your sisters to protect them."

"It's the only way," he says miserably. *"I've thought about it a lot. I'm going to hang up now."*

The line goes dead. I stare at my computer screen. Nova has written the intro for the next song. I make no attempt to hide the anger in my voice when I read her words. *"This is for all you dads who believe it's your way or the doorway: Waylon Jennings with 'Only Daddy That'll Walk the Line.'"*

As Waylon delivers his warning to the woman who's been stepping on his toes, I bury my face in my hands. Nova's on the talkback immediately. "We've caught a break. The police were able to trace 1121's call."

CHAPTER EIGHT

The tension drains from my body, but the relief doesn't last. I try to imagine how the cops will handle the situation. There are no good options. The time for the police psychologist is long past. Loser1121 is walking a razor-thin wire. If the police storm the house where he lives, the shock will knock him off the wire. Once he hits the ground, he'll move quickly. He'll kill until the cops bring him down.

Sometimes when we have a truly desperate caller, I can find a way to connect by putting myself in his place. I close my eyes and imagine myself in 1121's head. I can feel the walls closing in. Panic rises in my throat. I can't get air into my lungs. It's too much. I open my eyes, pick up the picture of Lily, focus on the moment when she held the dandelion and force myself to breathe deeply.

I'm in control again, but I can't forget 1121. Lily holds the dandelion as if were a magician's wand. Loser1121 was once a boy who knew the enchantment of dande- lions. He shouldn't have to face the end of his life alone. Through my earphones, I hear Waylon Jennings delivering the final warning to his wayward wife. In seconds I'll be back on the air. I call Nova on the talkback. "What's 1121's phone number?"

"It's on your screen," she says. "I sent it as soon as the police traced the call, but Charlie, the number was a dead end. It belongs to a woman named Mavis Durant here in the city."

I look at the blueprint 1121 sent in. "The surname of his family starts with a *K*. The initials don't fit," I say.

"Neither does anything else," Nova says. Her voice is bleak. She knows we've reached the end of the road. "Charlie, Mavis is eighty-three years old. She lives in a retirement home here in the city. The police are on their way to talk to her, but they believe the story she told them when they called her."

"What did she tell them?"

"That one day last month, she left her purse on a bench in the park by the legislature. The purse was turned in. There was nothing missing but her cellular phone. She didn't report it because the phone had been a gift from her grandson and she didn't want him to think she'd been careless."

"And she didn't cut off the service?"

"No. She said she never used the phone anyway. The phone company's records bear out her story. The phone wasn't used until tonight."

"Loser1121 was saving it," I say. "I'm going to call him."

"I'd better check with my friends in blue about that," Nova says. Her exchange with them is brief. She's back on the phone almost immediately. "They say go ahead and place the call. We haven't got anything else."

Since they arrived, the cops in the control room haven't had much to do but look stern and alert. Finally, there's at least the possibility of action. As I tap in the number, they spring to life, but apparently 1121 has turned off his cell. I give Nova and the officers the thumbs-down sign. My bag of tricks is empty. I flip on my microphone. I don't have to cast around for an effective tone. The urgency in my voice is the real thing.

"My name is Charlie Dowhanuik. And you are listening to 'The World of Charlie D' on what, even for us, is a weird and scary night.

In the last few minutes, I've been talking with a troubled friend. We don't know his name or where he lives—he could be anywhere. The point is we have to find him, and we have to help him. He calls himself loser1121. If you have any idea who 1121 might be, email us at charlied@nationtv.com or text us. We want to leave the phone lines open in case he decides to call in.

"1121, I hope you're still with us. You have no idea how much I hope that you're still up in your room and that you stay there. I know right at this moment you feel your whole life sucks. But take my word for it, life has a way of getting better."

I check the control room to see how I'm doing. The faces of the cops are stony, but Nova gives me a small and encouraging smile, so I plow on.

"Your experience isn't unique. I didn't have a lousy relationship with my father—I didn't have any relationship with him.

65

"He was a big shot in politics, and he was never around. I tried everything to get him to pay attention to me. I wasn't an easy kid. I was born with a birthmark that covers half my face. In a weird way, being a freak was liberating. I had nothing to lose—so I took a lot of chances. My mother used to say that I didn't have friends, I had fans. Other kids hung around me just to see how far I was going to push it.

"What I'm trying to say is that I grew up fine without a father. You can too. There are people who can help you, 1121. I can help you. Just call. You have our number, 1-800-555-2333. Please just call."

CHAPTER NINE

I stare at the two rows of lights in front of me. Each row has eight lights— one for each phone line. The bottom light goes solid when Nova answers it. When she puts up the line for mc to take the call on air, thc top light goes solid. When we're going full tilt that means sixteen greenish-yellow lights are blinking at me. Tonight there's nothing. The lines are dead. The lights are dark.

Nova sends the intro for the next tune. I open my mike and announce the title on air.

"Here's Madonna with 'Papa Don't Preach.' If any of you out there can weave a connection between what our troubled friend is going through and 'Papa Don't Preach,' you can have my job."

Through my earphones, Madonna sings of an unmarried girl pleading with her father to accept her decision to keep her baby. I stare at the phone lines. The first three lines are for local callers. If 1121's call comes in on one of those lines, we might be able to get to him in time.

But the lines stay dark. Madonna's nearing the end of her song. I glance at the control room. It would be reassuring to make eye contact with Nova, but this isn't my night. And there's a new and unwelcome development. Howard Dowhanuik has come into the control room. My father has always dominated every room he enters, and the control room is no exception. He has the body of an aging linebacker—tall, somewhat stooped but still powerful. Suddenly even the cops seem small and vulnerable. My father says a few words to them, bends to speak to Nova and then bingo, he walks through the door to my studio.

I'm not in the mood for company. "What the hell are you doing here?"

He doesn't answer. He just moves toward my desk and stands there, towering over me.

"Get out," I say.

He locks eyes with me.

"Not until you hear what I have to say." His voice is deep, gruff and commanding— a good voice for a politician.

"Make it fast," I say. "I'm back on the air in fifteen seconds."

"I was listening to your show when I was at Nighthawks. I'm pretty sure I know who loser1121 is."

I open my talkback.

"Nova, Howard thinks he can identify…"

Nova is curt.

"He told us. I'll keep playing music till you're ready to go back on air." She pauses. When she speaks again, I can feel her anxiety. "Charlie, don't let your feelings about Howard get in the way. He's all we've got."

I turn to my father.

"Okay. Shoot."

Without being asked, Howard takes the chair we use for guest experts.

"Is there any information you're not making public?" he asks.

I open the email note from 1121. After my father reads it, I open the attachments—the picture of the carving knife and finally the blueprint with 1121's route marked out. I turn to Howard.

"Does this fit what you know?"

"It fits." My father picks up the newspaper I bought at the drugstore, folds it so he's looking at the photo of the political

Rising Star and his family. Howard's hands are rough—the hands of a man who still likes to chop his own wood and maintain his own vehicles. His forefinger taps the picture of the boy staring down at the picnic table. "That's 1121," he says. "Josh James Kirkwood. I don't know the girls' names, but the mother's name is Marion." Howard moves his forefinger to the image of the Rising Star. "You'll recognize this prick. He's the man destiny has sent to save my party from itself—Josh Kirkwood."

I take the newspaper from him and stare at the picture.

"How did you make the connection?"

My father massages the back of his neck. It's the same thing I do when I'm tense.

"There was a meeting at Kirkwood's house a couple of weeks ago," he says. "I've been shooting off my mouth about how much I hate the direction the party's going in, so I guess they were hoping to win me over.

It didn't work. Kirkwood is a self-righteous, condescending asshole. He was pissing me off, so I left. I was getting into my car when the kid came running after me and asked me if I was your father. I said I was, and the kid—Josh—said that I must be really proud of you."

"What did you say?"

My father is used to answering tough questions, but this time, he hesitates.

"I said that I didn't know you."

I thought I was past being hurt by this man, but apparently not.

"At least you didn't lie," I say.

My father moves closer. I can smell his aftershave. In the days when he was drinking heavily, he used to drench himself in it. For a kid, it was overpowering, but tonight I find the scent surprisingly comforting.

"There's more," he says. "Josh said I should get to know you because you were a really great person."

"So we know that Josh's not much of a judge of character," I say tightly.

My father pounds the table with his fist.

"God damn it, Charlie, this isn't about you and me. This is about Josh." He picks up the earphones on the desk in front of him and puts them on. "Turn on our mikes. Let's do what we need to do."

I flick on our microphones and lean into mine. My voice is tense.

"*We have a guest—Howard Dowhanuik, a political legend in our time, and my father. Howard and I are going to talk about what it's like for a boy to grow up in his father's shadow.*"

My father's been staring at his hands, but when he hears my words, his massive head jerks up.

"*Politics was just my job. I never made a big deal of who I was.*"

"*You didn't have to,*" I say. "*There were people who did it for you. You were always surrounded by hangers-on, telling you how*

73

terrific you were, how brilliant your last speech was, how the country would fall apart if you didn't win the next election. You were always away—righting wrongs and drying every tear."

"It wasn't that bad," he says quietly. "I was around. Besides, you didn't need me. You had a lot of friends."

"They weren't friends. They were kids who wanted to catch my act—see how high I'd go or how fast I'd drive or how many chances I'd take. Everybody noticed me except the one I wanted to notice me."

Howard looks dumbfounded.

"Is that really what all that crazy behavior was about?"

I grab his arm.

"It wasn't crazy behavior. I wanted you to pay attention. I wanted you to look at me. I wanted you to really see me. 1121, I hope you're listening. This isn't an act. This is the truth. I know how you feel. I know what it's like to be lost in your father's shadow."

My voice breaks. *"I know what it's like to have a father who's larger than life."*

Howard's eyes are hooded.

"I wasn't larger than life. I was a scared Ukrainian kid who earned his way through university playing football. I ran hard because I was afraid that if I ever stopped running, people would see that I was nothing special."

My father and I lock eyes. I wonder if this is the first time either of us has ever really seen the other. We both earn our living with words, but suddenly neither of us seems to have anything to say. More dead air.

Howard is the first to speak. *"Do you remember the time I took you to see* The Wizard of Oz? *You were just a little guy. You got scared and crawled up on my knee."*

"I remember," I say.

"You were scared of the Wizard because he was so powerful and he had such a big voice," my father says. *"But I told you to keep*

watching because Dorothy's little dog was going to do something that would show you the Wizard wasn't anything to be afraid of."

"And I stayed on your knee and watched," I say, remembering. "Toto pulled down the curtain, and I saw that the Wizard wasn't really scary at all. He was just a little man doing tricks with a bunch of wheels and levers."

I turn toward the control room. Nova and the cops are as motionless as figures in a wax museum. We're all waiting. I move close to my microphone. I drop my voice to a whisper.

"Don't be fooled, 1121. Don't let your life be ruined by something that isn't real."

My father and I exchange a look. Then we both turn our eyes to the board with the lights that indicate the status of the phone lines. The board is still dark. We watch together, willing the call from Josh. Finally there's a yellow-green flicker in the bottom light of line one. It's a local call. The top light goes solid. Nova's put up the line for me to take on air.

My father and I both reach for our earphones. We hear Josh's voice, small and scared. *"I don't want people to know who I am,"* he says.

The top button goes dark. "You're off air now, Josh," I say. "We can talk."

"You know who I am," he says. He sounds scared. "I don't want anybody to find out what I was planning to do."

"Nobody's going to find out anything," my father says. "Charlie and I will meet you whenever you want. Wherever you'll feel safe."

"I want to talk to you now," he says. "Everyone's sleeping. I can come down the back stairs and meet you in the alley behind our house."

"Okay," I say. "I'll be right there."

"We'll be right there," my father says. "I've got my car here, and I know where

Josh lives. It's going to be all right, son," he says. He reaches out and touches my arm. In that moment, I know that he's speaking not just to Josh but to me.

"Could you do me a favor?" Josh asks.

"Name it," I say.

"Could you bring me a Big Gulp from 7-Eleven?"

"Coke?"

"Yeah. Thanks, Charlie." His laugh is small and sad. "You always know what people need."

CHAPTER TEN

When the police psychologist offers to come with us to meet Josh, she doesn't have to ask twice. Howard and I have seen Josh's blueprints. We know his demons are powerful and that we'll need an ally.

Dr. Elizabeth Lu is a broad-faced woman with a calming manner and shrewd eyes. She knows my father and I are on edge, so she waits for us to open the conversation.

Howard still drives his old gas-guzzling Buick. Dr. Lu takes the backseat, leaving me to ride shotgun. Behind us, an unmarked car carrying four of our city's finest follows at a discreet distance. It's a hot night, and the car doesn't have air-conditioning, so we drive with the windows down, listening to the music Nova has chosen to finish the show.

The mood in the old Buick is tense. We are all focused on the same question. My father, always the man of action, poses it.

"How do we handle this?" he asks.

Dr. Lu's answer is simple and sensible.

"Follow Josh's lead," she says.

As we turn onto Josh's street, Nova comes on air for the sign-off. She has a beautiful voice for radio—warm and husky—but she doesn't like being on air, so she stays on her side of the glass. We always end our show by talking about what, if anything, we've learned that night.

Nova follows the pattern.

"So what have we learned on our Father's Day show?" she asks. As soon as I hear her voice, my pulse slows. *"Maybe the one lesson we've learned is that in the end what matters is not who your father is but who you think he is. Charlie has a favorite quote. 'Forgive yourself for being human.' Maybe on this Father's Day weekend, we should all try to forgive our dads for being human."*

When we turn into the alley behind Josh's house, the air is fragrant with the scent of nicotiana. We park and walk toward the small figure waiting by the garage. Josh is wearing shorts and a T-shirt. He has a mop of dark hair. He looks very young and very fragile.

The light from the garage glints off the blade of the carving knife he has clasped in his hand. I'm holding the Big Gulp. My father doesn't hesitate. He extends his hand palm up.

"You'll need both hands to hold your drink, Josh," he says.

Josh passes him the carving knife.

"Is it over?" Josh asks.

"This part of it is," I say. "You've met my father. This is Doctor Lu. She's here to help."

Josh sips his drink, then looks up at Doctor Lu.

"My mum has wanted me to get help for a long time. She has a doctor lined up and everything."

"Maybe that doctor and I can work together," Doctor Lu says. Her voice is gentle and reassuring.

"Two of you and my mother and me. That's four against one," Josh says, and he sounds hopeful.

We stay with him until he finishes his Big Gulp. He puts the cup in the recycle bin in front of the garage and opens the gate. Dr. Lu follows him.

"I'd like to talk to your mum tonight. If that's okay with you."

"It's okay," he says, "but what if he tries to stop us?"

"We'll make him understand," Dr. Lu says. She points to the unmarked police car up the alley. "Josh, there are four officers in that car. Their job is to take care of your mum and us."

Josh nods.

"That's good," he says. Then he and Dr. Lu cross the yard and move toward his house.

When he speaks, Howard's voice is thick with emotion.

"Do you think Josh is going to make it?"

"I hope so," I say. "His chances are better than they were when the night started."

The unmarked police car pulls up behind the Buick. I go over and tell the officers that Doctor Lu has gone into the house with Josh and that he seems calm and optimistic. The constable behind the wheel thanks me. My father hands the constable the carving knife, and we walk to the car. For the first time that night, the tension that has been pressing down on me like a weight is lifted. Howard and I exchange a glance, and then, in unison, we exhale.

CHAPTER ELEVEN

I call Nova from the car.

"Josh has just taken the first step," I say. "He and Dr. Lu have gone into his house to talk to Josh's mother. It's a beginning."

Nova's voice is tight.

"It could have been an ending. Charlie, I was so scared."

"Howard and I listened to you on the way over. You sounded great."

Her laugh is strained.

"Fake it until you make it," she says. "But I'm going to stick to the control room. I don't have to fake it there."

"You're the best producer in the business," I say.

"And I still have a job," Nova says. "So do you. Henry Burgh called a few minutes ago. He made Evan an offer for CVOX that Evan couldn't refuse. And guess who our new boss is? Misty de Vol. Henry is giving Misty CVOX as a wedding gift."

I laugh. "Now that is kick-ass news. Howard and I are going for coffee. Want us to swing by and pick you up?"

"Thanks," she says. "But I think your coffee date with Howard should be a father-son thing."

"You're probably right," I say. "Howard and I have a lot of ground to cover."

* * *

When we pull out of the alley, my father turns on the radio, and we hear "Cat's in the Cradle" again. We listen to Harry Chapin's sweet melodic voice without speaking.

When the song is over, Howard says, "That's a good song. Did he write anything else?"

"Nothing anybody remembers," I say. "He was killed in a car accident when he was thirty-eight years old."

"We never know how much time we have, do we?" Howard says.

"No," I say. "We never know." And then I reach over and touch my father's hand.

The Shadow Killer is GAIL BOWEN's third title in the Rapid Reads series, all featuring late-night radio talk-show host Charlie D. Her other titles in the series are *Love You to Death* and *One Fine Day You're Gonna Die.* Gail's bestselling mystery series featuring Joanne Kilbourn now numbers an even dozen titles with the publication of *The Nesting Dolls* (2010).

RAPID READS

The following is an excerpt from
Love You To Death, another exciting
Rapid Reads novel by Gail Bowen.

978-1-55469-262-0 $9.95 pb

**Someone is killing some of Charlie D's
favorite listeners.**

Charlie D is the host of a successful late-night radio
call-in show that offers supportive advice to troubled
listeners. *Love You to Death* takes place during one
installment of "The World According to Charlie D"—
two hours during which Charlie must discover who
is killing some of the most vulnerable members of
his audience.

CHAPTER ONE

A wise man once said 90 percent of life is just showing up. An hour before midnight, five nights a week, fifty weeks a year, I show up at CVOX radio. Our studios are in a concrete-and-glass box in a strip mall. The box to the left of us sells discount wedding dresses. The box to the right of us rents XXX movies. The box where I work sells talk radio—"ALL TALK/ALL THE TIME." Our call letters are on the roof. The *O* in CVOX is an open, red-lipped mouth with a tongue that looks like Mick Jagger's.

After I walk under Mick Jagger's tongue, I pass through security, make my way down the hall and slide into a darkened booth. I slip on my headphones and adjust the microphone. I spend the next two hours trying to convince callers that life is worth living. I'm good at my job—so good that sometimes I even convince myself.

My name is Charlie Dowhanuik. But on air, where we can all be who we want to be, I'm known as Charlie D. I was born with my mother's sleepy hazel eyes and clever tongue, my father's easy charm, and a wine-colored birthmark that covers half my face. In a moment of intimacy, the only woman I've ever loved, now, alas, dead, touched my cheek and said, "You look as if you've been dipped in blood."

One of the very few people who don't flinch when they look at my face is Nova ("Proud to Be Swiss") Langenegger.

For nine years, Nova has been the producer of my show, "The World According to Charlie D." She says that when she looks at me she doesn't see my birthmark—all she sees is the major pain in her ass.

Tonight when I walk into the studio, she narrows her eyes at me and taps her watch. It's a humid night and her blond hair is frizzy. She has a zit on the tip of her nose. She's wearing a black maternity T-shirt that says *Believe It or Not, I Used to Be Hot.*

"Don't sell yourself short, Mama Nova," I say. "You're still hot. Those hormones that have been sluicing through your body for nine months give you a very sexy glow."

"That's not a sexy glow," she says. "That's my blood pressure spiking. We're on the air in six minutes. I've been calling and texting you for two hours. Where were you?"

I open my knapsack and hand her a paper bag that glistens with grease from the onion rings inside. "There was a lineup at Fat Boy's," I say.

Nova shakes her head. "You always know what I want." She slips her hand into the bag, extracts an onion ring and takes a bite. Usually this first taste gives her a kid's pleasure, but tonight she chews on it dutifully. It might as well be broccoli. "Charlie, we need to talk," she says. "About Ian Blaise."

"He calls in all the time," I say. "He's doing fine. Seeing a shrink. Back to work part-time. Considering that it's only been six months since his wife and daughters were killed in that car accident, his recovery is a miracle."

Nova has lovely eyes. They're as blue as a northern sky. When she laughs, the skin around them crinkles. It isn't crinkling now. "Ian jumped from the roof of his apartment building Saturday," she says. "He's dead."

I feel as if I've been kicked in the stomach. "He called me at home last week. We talked for over an hour."

Nova frowns. "We've been over this a hundred times. You shouldn't give out your home number. It's dangerous."

"Not as dangerous as being without a person you can call in the small hours," I say tightly. "That's when the ghoulies and ghosties and long-leggedy beasties can drive you over the edge. I remember the feeling well."

"The situation may be more sinister than that, Charlie," Nova says. "This morning someone sent us Ian's obituary. This index card was clipped to it."

Nova hands me the card. It's the kind school kids use when they have to make a speech in class. The message is neatly printed, and I read it aloud. "'Ian Blaise wasn't worth your time, Charlie. None of them are. They're cutting off your oxygen.

I'm going to save you.'" I turn to Nova. "What the hell is this?"

"Well, for starters, it's the third in a series. Last week someone sent us Marcie Zhang's obituary."

"The girl in grade nine who was being bullied," I say. "You didn't tell me she was dead."

"There's a lot I don't tell you," Nova says. She sounds tired. "Anyway, there was a file card attached to the obituary. The message was the same as this one—minus the part about saving you. That's new."

"I don't get it," I say. "Marcie Zhang called in a couple of weeks ago. Remember? She was in great shape. She'd aced her exams. And she had an interview for a job as a junior counselor at a summer camp."

"I remember. I also remember that the last time James Washington called in, he said that he was getting a lot of support from other gay athletes who'd been outed, and he wished he'd gone public sooner."

"James is dead too?"

Nova raises an eyebrow. "Lucky you never read the papers, huh? James died as a result of a hit-and-run a couple of weeks ago. We got the newspaper clipping with the index card attached. Same message—word for word—as the one with Marcie's obituary."

"And you never told me?"

"I didn't connect the dots, Charlie. A fourteen-year-old girl who, until very recently has been deeply disturbed, commits suicide. A professional athlete is killed in a tragic accident. Do you have any idea how much mail we get? How many calls I handle a week? Maybe I wasn't as sharp as I should have been, because I'm preoccupied with this baby. But this morning after I got Ian's obituary—with the extended-play version of the note—I called the police."

I snap. "You called the cops? Nova, you and I have always been on the same side of that particular issue. The police operate in a black-and-white world. Right/wrong. Guilty/innocent. Sane/Not so much. We've always agreed that life is more complex for our listeners. They tell us things they can't tell anybody else. They have to trust us."

Nova moves so close that her belly is touching mine. Her voice is low and grave. "Charlie, this isn't about a lonely guy who wants you to tell him it's okay to have a cyberskin love doll as his fantasy date. There's a murderer out there. A real murderer—not one of your Goth death groupies. We can't handle this on our own."

I reach over and rub her neck. "Okay, Mama Nova, you win. But over a hundred thousand people listen to our show every night. Where do we start?"

Nova gives my hand a pat and removes it from her neck. "With you, Charlie," she says. "The police want to use our show to flush out the killer."

RAPID READS

The following is an excerpt from
One Fine Day You're Gonna Die, another
exciting Rapid Reads novel by Gail Bowen.

978-1-55469-337-5 $9.95 pb

It will take all of Charlie D's skills to
keep this Halloween from being another
"Day of the Dead."

Charlie D is back doing his late-night radio call-in
show. It's Halloween—The Day of the Dead.
His studio guest this evening is Dr. Robin Harris,
an arrogant and ambitious "expert in the arts of dying
and grieving." Charlie and Dr. Harris do not hit it
off. Things go from bad to worse when the doctor's
ex-lover goes on air to announce that he's about to
end his life.

CHAPTER ONE

Tonight as I was riding my bike to the radio station where I do the late-night call-in show, a hearse ran a light and plowed into me. I swerved. The vehicle clipped my back wheel, and I flew through the air to safety. My Schwinn was not so lucky. The hearse skidded to a stop. The driver jumped out, sprinted over and knelt beside me on the wet pavement. "Are you all right?" he asked.

I checked my essentials.

"As all right as I'll ever be," I said.

The man bent closer. The streetlight illuminated both our faces. He looked like the actor who played Hawkeye on the old TV show *M*A*S*H*. His brow furrowed with concern when he saw my cheek.

"You're bleeding," he said.

"It's a birthmark," I said.

As birthmarks go, mine is a standout. It covers half my face, like a blood mask. Nine out of ten strangers turn away when they see it. This man moved in closer.

"The doctors weren't able to do anything?" he asked.

"Nope."

"But you've learned to live with it."

"Most of the time," I said.

"That's all any of us can do," the man said, and he grinned. His smile was like Hawkeye's—open and reassuring. He offered his hand and pulled me to my feet. "I'll take you wherever you want to go," he said.

He picked up my twisted Schwinn and stowed it in the back of the hearse. I slid into the passenger seat. The air inside was cool, flower-scented and oddly soothing. After we'd buckled our seat belts, the man turned the keys in the ignition.

"Where to?" he asked.

"CVOX Radio," I said. "728 Shuter."

"It's in a strip mall," he said. "Between a store that sells discount wedding dresses and a place that rents x-rated movies."

"I'm impressed," I said. "This is a big city."

"It is," he agreed. "But my business involves pick up and delivery. I need to know where people are."

Perhaps because the night was foggy and he'd already had one accident, the driver didn't talk as he threaded his way through the busy downtown streets. When we turned on to Shuter, I saw the neon call letters on the roof of our building. The *O* in CVOX ("ALL TALK/ALL THE TIME") is an open mouth with red lips and a tongue that looks like Mick Jagger's. Fog had fuzzed the brilliant scarlet neon of Mick's tongue to a soft pink. It looked like the kiss a woman leaves on a tissue when she blots her lipstick.

"I'll pick you up when your show's over," the man said.

"I'll take a cab," I said. "But thanks for the offer."

He shrugged and handed me a business card. "Call me if you change your mind. Otherwise, I'll courier a cheque to you tomorrow to pay for your bike."

"You don't know my name."

The man flashed me his Hawkeye smile. "Sure I do. Your name is Charlie Dowhanuik and you're the host of 'The World According to Charlie D.' I'm a fan. I even phoned in once. It was the night you walked off the show and disappeared for a year. You were in rough shape."

"That's why I left."

"I was relieved that you did," he said. "I sensed that if you didn't turn things around, you and I were destined to meet professionally. My profession, not yours. You were too young to need my services, so I called in to remind you of what Woody Allen said."

"I remember. 'Life is full of misery, loneliness and suffering and it's over much too soon.'" I met the man's eyes. "Wise words," I said. "I still ponder them."

"So you haven't stopped grieving for the woman you lost?"

"Nope."

"But you decided to keep on living," he said.

"For the time being," I said. We shook hands, and I opened the car door and climbed out. As I watched the hearse disappear into the fog, the opening lines of an old schoolyard rhyme floated to the top of my consciousness.

Do you ever think when a hearse goes by
That one fine day you're gonna die?
They'll wrap you up in a cotton sheet
And throw you down about forty feet.
The worms crawl in,
The worms crawl out...

There was more, but I had to cut short my reverie. It was October 31. Halloween. The Day of the Dead. And I had a show to do.